Leroy Is Missing

Another Sam and Dave Mystery Story

The Case of the Sabotaged School Play

Leroy

Is Missing

Marilyn Singer

ILLUSTRATED BY

JUDY GLASSER

Harper & Row, Publishers

New York

Special thanks to Ira Brustein
for the information on horse racing
and to Steve Parton for his collaboration

Library of Congress Cataloging in Publication Data
Singer, Marilyn.
  Leroy is missing.

  Summary: Hot on the trail of the missing Leroy O'Toole,
detectives Sam and Dave Bean stumble onto an illegal operation.
  [1. Mystery and detective stories] I. Glasser, Judy,
ill. II. Title.
PZ7.S6172Le 1984   [Fic]   83-48441
ISBN 0-06-025796-2
ISBN 0-06-025797-0 (lib. bdg.)

Designed by Constance Fogler
1 2 3 4 5 6 7 8 9 10
First Edition

Leroy Is Missing

1

"Even a famous detective like Sam Bean can mess up," Dave Bean gasped. He was running hard to keep up with his twin brother. It wasn't easy; Sam was athletic, while Dave was not. "Mom'll get over it—even though you totally ruined her beaded sweater by throwing it in the washing machine."

"It was stained," Sam mumbled, and ran harder. How come Dave never does anything wrong, he wondered.

"Hey, come on. You know I can't run that fast!"

"For a famous detective you're awfully out of shape!" Sam called over his shoulder.

"Hey, look out!" Dave cried.

Too late. Sam turned his head just in time to see the front wheel of the dirt bike crash into his leg, sending him and the rider into a heap on the road.

"Sam, are you okay?" Dave shouted.

"*Owww!* You creep! You made me fall!" hollered the rider, a red-haired, freckled kid of about eight.

Sam limped to his feet. "I'm all right," he called back to Dave. He wasn't really. His knees and elbows were bruised and he had a cut on his hand.

Leroy Is Missing

But the kid was younger and smaller than he, so he hobbled over to him and asked, "Where are you hurt?"

The kid pointed to his bike. "Look at this! You scratched the finish! I'll sue you!"

Sam stared at the bike and then at the boy. There wasn't a scratch on *him*. For one second, Sam wanted to haul off and deck him, but Dave, who'd caught up with them, said, "Listen, kid. If anyone's gonna sue, it's us. This accident was your fault. You're not supposed to ride along this path. It's for pedestrians."

The kid looked from Sam to Dave and then back to Sam and shook his head as if to clear it. "Hey, I'm seeing double. Concussion! I've got a concussion!"

"You're going to have one if you don't get out of here," Sam muttered.

"What's your name, kid?" Dave said, pulling a pad out of his hip pocket. "In case we do sue."

The kid gave them a tough look. "Leroy. Spelled L-E-R-O-Y. And I don't care if you do sue, 'cause I'm gonna tell my dad and he's going to beat you up." Then he got on his bike and rode away.

"Man," said Sam. "I hope I don't see him around in a big hurry."

"Yeah," agreed Dave. "But doesn't he remind you of someone?"

Leroy Is Missing

"Who?"

"That red-haired girl in our class, Rita O'Toole."

Sam thought about it and gave a little smile. There was a slight resemblance, but Rita O'Toole was the smartest kid in their class and she seemed nice, too, not like the obnoxious jerk who'd just crippled him. He shook his head. "Nah. No way," he said, "No way!"

2

Two hours later, in an attempt to make his mother like him a little more, Sam was vacuuming the house. Dave had helped him hobble home and there they found a note. It read:

> *Gone clothes shopping.*
> *Don't iron my leather coat or*
> *soak Dad's bowling shoes.*
> *Mom*

Dave snickered and Sam gave him a dirty look.

"Oh, come on. It *is* pretty funny," Dave said.

"Ha-ha," said Sam.

"Look, it's Saturday and I don't intend to do

5

any homework. Want to help me with my model Model A?"

"No thanks."

Dave shrugged and went upstairs while Sam sat and thought for a while. Why can't I do things right like Dave, he wondered. After he got tired of wondering, he tried to read the newspaper. POST OFFICE TO GET NEW PLANTINGS. CRACKDOWN ON BOOK-IES. MEAT PRICES UP. KILLERDILLER GANG STRIKES AGAIN. The headlines made him sleepy, so he took a nap. And after the nap, he started vacuuming.

He was halfway finished with the living room when the doorbell rang. "I'll get it," he hollered up to Dave.

Sam turned off the machine and tripped over the cord. Wincing, because he'd hurt his leg again, he opened the door.

And there, red-haired, bespectacled and looking very serious, was Rita O'Toole.

"Hello," she said. "Am I disturbing you?"

"N-no," Sam stammered—something he did when he was surprised.

"I'm Rita. Rita O'Toole," she said.

"I kn-know. I'm…"

"Wait. Don't tell me. Just smile."

At that, Sam grinned. Rita O'Toole wasn't known as the smartest kid in the class for nothing.

Leroy Is Missing

"You're Sam. You have a chipped front tooth and Dave doesn't. Otherwise, you look exactly alike—just about. But your personalities are different."

"Yeah? Tell me how..."

"Later. Right now I'm here on business. Urgent business. Can I come in?"

"Oh, sure," Sam said, realizing that all this time he'd been blocking the doorway.

Rita entered the living room, looked around and sat down on the couch. "I'll wait here. You get your brother."

Sam didn't ask why. He just ran upstairs to fetch Dave. Then the two of them hopped back downstairs in a flash.

"Hello," said Dave. "What's all this about?"

"This is about my younger brother. Three hours ago my mother sent him to do some errands and then she went to visit some friends. He was supposed to be back by now, but he hasn't returned."

"Well, did you check the places he went to?" asked Dave. He was always able to ask intelligent questions like that.

"No, not yet. I thought you both would help me."

"Why us?"

"Because you two are famous detectives, aren't you? That's what everyone in school says. You solved the 'Case of the Sabotaged School Play' and the 'Forged Lottery Tickets Fracas' and others, too."

8

Leroy Is Missing

"Well, that's true. We did. But what makes you think your brother's a 'case' just because he hasn't come home yet?" Dave asked.

"That's a good question. And it deserves a good answer. The reason I think something serious is going on is because my brother took his bike with him, and an hour ago, Jason Rothberg brought it home. He said he found it lying on its side in that little park off Tremont Street."

"So? Couldn't your brother have left it there?"

Rita smiled. "You don't know my brother, Dave. If there's anything Leroy loves it's that bike. He'd never leave it like that."

"Did you say Leroy?" Sam asked.

"Yes. He's eight and looks a lot like me."

Sam looked at Dave and groaned. "I hope he stays lost," he muttered.

"What was that?" asked Rita.

"Nothing," Dave said, poking Sam. "We'll help you find him, Rita. Do you know where he might have gone first?"

"Yes. The post office. He had a package to mail and he'd want to get rid of that first."

"Good. Let's start there," said Dave.

He and Rita left the house together and Sam, frowning, followed them and thought, At least wherever that squirt is, he's not mowing down anyone else with his bike.

9

Leroy Is Missing

3

The post office was locked when they got there ("I forgot—it closes early on Saturday," said Dave), but they noticed one car still in the parking lot. So they pounded on the glass door of the office until a woman's face appeared in a window, shook its head, mouthed the word "Closed" and disappeared.

"That's not Ms. Braswell. It must be a new clerk," said Dave. "Oh, well. Bang on it again."

This time, the sour face attached to a short figure dressed all in gray came to the door. "We're closed," she yelled, pointing at the sign.

"We know," Dave yelled back. "But it's important!"

The postal clerk frowned, shook her head and disappeared once more.

"What do we do now?" asked Sam. "Break down the door?"

Dave thought a minute. Then he pulled out his notepad and wrote on a piece of paper: LEROY O'TOOLE IS MISSING. WE NEED INFORMATION. "Okay everybody," he said. "Let's wake up Old Sourpuss."

So they all beat on the door once again until the

clerk angrily came to the window once more. "If you don't go away, I'll call the police," she yelled, and turned red.

Dave held up the note.

The clerk read it, then looked at Dave, Sam and finally Rita.

"He's my brother!" hollered Rita.

The clerk nodded, held up a finger meaning "Wait a minute," disappeared and then showed up at the door, which she opened. "Now," she said, in a nasal voice, "what's all this about?"

"It's about Rita's brother," Dave said. "He was supposed to be home hours ago and he hasn't shown up, but a kid found his bike abandoned in the park. We're talking to people who might have seen him."

"Is he a short kid with a loud mouth like hers?" the woman said, nodding at Rita.

"That's him, all right," muttered Sam.

"He was here about two hours ago. Had a big package to mail. There was a long line and he got impatient and knocked over a couple of signs and things."

Afraid to look at Rita, Sam and Dave looked at each other.

"That sounds like Leroy. He's a real pest," Rita said.

"Then what do you want him back for?" Sam

muttered, and Dave, stifling a chuckle, kicked him.

"Anyway, his—your—father was nice. Helped pick the stuff up."

"My father?" Rita exclaimed. "He's visiting some friends."

"Oh. Must have been your uncle then. The man Leroy was with. He was the paternal type."

"Our uncle? None of our uncles are in town."

Sam and Dave looked at each other again.

"What did the man look like?" Dave asked.

"Nothing special. Medium height. Brown hair. I didn't really look closely at him. He and Leroy left together, but that's all I can tell you."

Sam sighed, but Dave said, "Thank you, ma'am. You've been a great help." And he ushered Sam and Rita out of the post office.

"A man Old Sourpuss thought was our uncle! I don't like this. I don't like it one bit," said Rita.

Neither do I, thought Sam.

"Let's not jump to any conclusions," said Dave. "What's the next stop on your list?"

"Well, I would guess Dinker's Deli because it's right near here."

"Okay, then Dinker's Deli it is," Dave said.

Leroy Is Missing

4

Dinker's Deli was not owned by Mr. Dinker. He had sold it twenty-two years ago to Mr. Treebottom, who thought Dinker's Deli sounded better than Treebottom's Deli. Mr. Treebottom was a very nice man whom everyone liked. His only problem was that he was very nearsighted and he had the unfortunate habit of putting his face very close to a person's to find out who he or she was. Which was just what he was doing to Sam at that moment. "Why it's one of the Bean twins, isn't it?"

"Yes, Mr. Treebottom," Sam said, trying to focus his eyes, which were crossing because Mr. Treebottom's nose was practically touching his own.

"Which one are you?"

"Sam."

"Then this must be Dave," Mr. Treebottom said, giving Dave the same close-eyed treatment and Sam a chance to refocus his eyes. Sam glanced at the small TV set behind the counter. It was on although the sound wasn't and a man with bushy eyebrows was demonstrating yo-yo tricks. Sam watched him perform a simple one called "Around the World," then turned his attention back to Mr. Treebottom.

"But who's this boy?" the grocer was saying. "Looks like...Oh, pardon me, Rita O'Toole. I mistook you for your brother. He was in earlier."

Rita took off her glasses, wiped the steam from Mr. Treebottom's breath off them and said, "He was? When was he here?"

"About two hours ago, I'd say. Bought milk, coleslaw, a pound of bologna and a giant Hershey bar."

"The Hershey bar wasn't on Mom's shopping list," Rita muttered.

"Is something wrong? You sound upset."

"Leroy hasn't come home yet. He left his bike in the park. We're worried that something might have happened to him," Dave said.

"How do you know he isn't home?" Mr. Treebottom asked.

"What do you mean?"

"You're not home. He might have shown up by now."

"But the bike..."

"Maybe someone swiped it, then dumped it."

"Gee, you may be right," Rita said. "I'll call." She dashed out to a pay phone.

Sam was torn. He wanted to keep her company. But he also wanted to stay and find out if Mr. Treebottom had any clues in case Leroy was still missing. He decided to stay.

Leroy Is Missing

"Was Leroy alone, Mr. Treebottom?" Dave was asking.

"No. He was with a fellow he called Uncle Doug. Funny, I didn't...uh...see him too well, but he looked somehow...familiar, this Uncle Doug. Don't know why. Anyway, they were talking about going over the mountain."

"The mountain? What mountain?"

"Don't know. Sure aren't any mountains near here. The nearest one is a hundred miles away."

Sam felt a chill go up his back. He expected that Dave did too, but his brother was acting cool.

"And they left together?" Dave said.

"Yep."

A sound made them all turn. It was Rita. She shook her head. "No answer."

Sam wanted to comfort her. He didn't know how, so he said awkwardly, "Uh...Rita, do you want some...uh...gum?"

"If Leroy shows up again, tell him to go straight home. Will you, Mr. Treebottom?" Dave said.

"Sure thing. And I'll bawl him out for making his sister worry."

Everyone—even Rita—had to smile. Mr. Treebottom couldn't even bawl out his dog when it chewed up his pipe.

When Rita and the twins got to the street, Dave said, "Well, Rita, we found out something. Leroy definitely wasn't alone. He left with Uncle Doug."

Rita stiffened. Then, after a pause, she said, "We don't have an Uncle Doug. We never did."

"I was afraid you were going to say that," said Dave.

And Sam let out a long, low whistle. Neither he nor Dave had the heart to tell Rita that her brother and his phoney uncle were planning a long trip.

5

Rita was trying to stay calm. Sam could practically hear her brain ticking away. She's a lot like Dave, he thought. She probably thinks he's the smart one and I'm the dumb one because I'm so quiet.

"We better stay on Leroy's trail," Rita said. "Maybe this Uncle Doug person is some friend of Leroy's. I don't know....Maybe..." She stopped and frowned.

"Or maybe he's a teacher or some kid's parent Leroy knows," Sam suggested a little shyly.

"Yeah, there may be a perfectly logical explanation," Dave agreed. "But I think you're right, Rita.

Leroy Is Missing

We better stay on Leroy's trail. Don't you think so, Sam?"

Sam nodded. If there wasn't a perfectly logical explanation, if Uncle Doug was up to no good and taking Leroy on a long trip over the mountain, they might not have left town yet. Maybe they were hanging out in a shop. Maybe they were even planning to finish Leroy's errands, go home and then leave.... No, that didn't make sense. But it *was* possible that someone else had seen them or even knew just where they were going.

"What's the next place on the list, then?" Dave asked.

"Kitty's," Rita said. Suddenly, she grinned. "I think he would have wanted to get that errand over fast."

"Kitty's? He had an errand to run there?" Dave said.

"Mom shops there. I've never been inside," Sam said at the same time.

"Yes. Well, now you will," Rita answered. And she grinned again.

"Is that Kitty?" Sam asked, cowering slightly as he peered through the window of the shop.

"That's her."

"Wow!"

Even Dave gulped. "Well....Let's be cool. Re-

19

member we have to interrogate her—she may be a witness.''

Sam just shook his head. The store was embarrassing enough—nightgowns and stockings and underwear on mannequins in the window. No wonder Leroy wanted to get whatever it was he had to do here over with fast. And on top of that, there was Kitty....

"Well, I guess she's not going to bite us. Let's go in," said Dave, holding open the door for Rita.

She grinned back at Sam and went in, followed by Dave and then Sam, who was turning pink aroung the ears.

Kitty, all six feet of her, tottered forward on three-inch spike heels. She set a white Angora cat on the counter and then patted her black, beehive hairdo to make sure not a strand was out of place (which could never happen anyway because she'd used nearly half a can of hair spray on it), opened her big, red lips and smiled. Dave started to speak, but was drowned out by Kitty's booming voice. "Hey, aren't you two cute. Identical twins. With a little girl friend...Why, it's Rita O'Toole. Just the person I wanted to see." She pronounced person like "poyson."

Dave winced and Sam shrank back, but Rita just asked, "What's the scoop, Kitty?"

"Your brother Leroy was here earlier. Scared Kitty

Leroy Is Missing

II over here practically to death.... You're all right now, precious, aren't you?" She stroked the cat, who yawned. "Then he gave me his order—a slip and three pairs of pantyhose. And left the package."

Dave winced again and Sam turned beet red.

"Here it is," Kitty finished, producing a pink and white paper bag with KITTY'S—FINE UNDER-GARMENTS AND HOSIERY written on it in bold, black letters.

"Thanks, Kitty. My mother will be glad to get it.... By the way, Leroy hasn't come home yet. Did he or his friend Doug tell you where they were going?"

"I didn't meet this Doug *poyson*—Leroy came in by himself. And I'm afraid I don't know where he went, but I can tell you he sure was in a hurry. He just gave me a note with his order and scooted out when Mrs. Blocknitz came in to buy a girdle."

I'd have scooted out then too, Sam thought, that is if I ever came in the first place.

"Okay. Thanks a lot, Kitty."

"You're welcome.... Here, be a gentleman and carry the bag for the lady." She winked at Rita and handed the bag to Sam. "Say, you boys, does your mother need any underwear?"

With the bag in his hand, Sam fled out of the store with Dave close at his heels. Rita, giggling, waved to Kitty and followed them slowly. It wasn't until they hit the street that Sam, about to give the bag to Rita, glanced down at it and noticed that someone had written two words on it: WIPE-OUT. LEROY. And someone had put a big black X next to Leroy's name.

"Wow," said Sam.

"Yeah. Wow," agreed Dave. "It's time for the Bean brothers to do some brainstorming."

Rita, pale but determined, said, "The Bean Brothers and Rita O'Toole."

6

"Hey, Sam," Tony said to Dave. "Long time, no see."

They were standing at the counter of Tony's Pizzeria. Rita had said that Leroy wasn't supposed to go there because he spent too much money on the games and also because their mother thought some funny characters hung out there, but that Leroy might have gone there anyway—especially after going to Kitty's. Sam understood. He sometimes hung out at Tony's, playing the machines and watching the oddballs who drifted in and out of the place, but Dave never did.

Leroy Is Missing

"Yeah," Dave said. "I've been busy."

Tony swiveled his head around to Sam, back to Dave, and then to Sam again. "I didn't know you had a twin. You guys could have quite a racket going if you wanted to."

"Yeah," Sam said again. "Hey, Tony, have you seen Leroy O'Toole today? We've been looking for him."

"Leroy? Nah. Not today," Tony said slowly. "I thought his mother doesn't want him to hang out here."

"She doesn't," answered Rita.

Tony shrugged and then asked them what kind of pie they wanted.

While they were sitting at a corner table, waiting for their pizza (double cheese, pepperoni and mushrooms, hold the onions), Dave, looking at the bag, said, "Okay. Brainstorming time. Who could've written this? Uncle Doug wasn't in the store."

"Unless Kitty's lying," said Rita.

"She might be. Then she'd be in on it," Dave mused. "There could be more people in on it too."

"It could be a gang," said Sam. He felt his mind slip into the same rhythm as Dave's—something that often happened between them, especially when they were working on a case together.

"Yeah," said Dave, tapping his fingers on the table. "But why would a gang—or anyone—want to

24

wipe out Leroy? What could he have done to make someone want to?"

I can think of a few things, thought Sam. But instead he said, "I don't know. Maybe...maybe he found out something he wasn't supposed to. You know, stumbled across something..."

"Ran into something, you mean," Dave said.

The two of them grinned at each other.

"Or maybe this isn't what we think it is," Dave said, pointing to the bag.

"Yeah, maybe. Hey, couldn't this be a code?" Sam said, beginning to get excited.

"No, I don't think so," Rita put in. "I know a lot about codes and this doesn't look like one.

"You do? Did you read a book about..." Sam began, but Dave interrupted him.

"*Psst*, look at that guy."

A man wearing a slouch hat over his eyes slouched his way toward the counter. He nodded at Tony. Tony nodded back and stood aside to let the man slouch into the back of the pizzeria. A minute later, a second man followed. Tony went back to punching dough as if nothing had happened.

"Weirdos is right," Rita said.

"I've seen that guy here before," Sam said.

"You have?" both Dave and Rita asked.

"Yeah. Once or twice. He always acts the same way."

Leroy Is Missing

Then a third man came in. "Wipe-out?" he asked Tony in a low voice.

Tony nodded and gestured to the back room.

Sam, Dave and Rita froze.

The man disappeared behind the counter.

"Oh, wow, we gotta get back there. They may have Leroy," Rita whispered.

"Yeah, but we can't just burst in," said Dave.

"Hey, kids, I'm just going around the back to throw out the garbage," Tony said. "Sam, how about you watch the place for me? You've done it before. And I'm not expecting any more...er... visitors."

"Oh, okay, Tony," Sam said.

Tony left, toting two big sacks.

"This is it. Quick, let's go listen at the door," Rita said.

They jumped to their feet and ran behind the counter. They put their ears to the door and listened hard, but they didn't hear a thing. Then, without warning the door swung open and revealed a flight of stairs leading down.

"Oh, wow," said Rita. "Let's go down the stairs."

"We better make it quick," said Dave.

"I'll go with you," Sam offered.

"No. Tony told you to watch the place. You stand guard. If you see him coming back, whistle."

"Why don't *you* stay here and mind the place?"

Leroy Is Missing

Sam said. "Tony doesn't know the difference between..."

But Dave and Rita were already down the steps. Then, before he could even pucker his lips, Sam heard the front door open. "Tony," he gasped. But it wasn't Tony at all. It was Kitty. And she was looking annoyed. "Listen, kid, where's your friend, Rita?" she said.

"Uh...um...she...went to...the...um..." Sam was trying to think up a good lie when Kitty noticed the bag from her store. She teetered over to it as fast as her three-inch heels would carry her. From her oversized handbag, she whipped out a little notepad and copied down the two words Sam had seen on the bag.

"Um...Rita went to the drugstore," he finally said.

"Well, I hope she got whatever she wanted there," Kitty replied. "Now, where's Tony?"

"He'll be back soon," Sam said. His head began to spin. Kitty wasn't leaving. Tony would be back any minute. If I whistle, he thought, Kitty will find out I'm lying. If I don't whistle....Maybe I should ask her right out who's going to wipe out Leroy and why. But then she might....What am I going to do?

And then Tony appeared. "Kitty, you almost didn't make it," he said. "They're starting in five."

Leroy Is Missing

"Here." Kitty shoved the paper at Tony.

He looked at it and nodded. Then Kitty shoved some bills his way.

"Wanna watch? I'm going to this time. It's gonna be a good one," Tony said.

Kitty shook her head. "No time. Let me know the good news."

Then Tony noticed Sam looking at him wide-eyed. "Listen, Sam, I'm closing up for a while now. You gotta go, okay?" He glanced around. "Where'd your brother and Leroy's sister go?"

"They...uh...left...and I...um...haven't finished my...um...pizza," Sam stammered.

"Take it with you, kid," Kitty said, propelling him out the door.

When he hit the street, he heard a click and turned to see the door of the pizzeria locked firmly behind him.

"See you, kid," Kitty said and tottered back up the street.

It was dark at the bottom of the steps. From behind the door there, Dave and Rita could smell

Leroy Is Missing

cigar smoke and hear the phone ringing and people talking. They pressed their ears against it and listened.

"How's Leroy gonna finish?" asked one voice.

"Forget Leroy. He's been scratched," answered another.

"Oh, no. We've got to go in there," Rita said.

"Hold on. They might..." Dave started to say. But before he could finish, the door swung open and he and Rita fell into the room.

"Well, well, well. What have we here?" someone said.

Two huge hands jerked them roughly to their feet, and Dave and Rita stared into an angry pair of eyes. They looked past the eyes and saw three other men with cigars arranged around a big television set in the center of the smoke-filled room.

"Didn't your mother ever teach you not to eavesdrop?" a small man in a chair said to them. The door opened again and Tony came in. "I just closed.... Uh-oh. I wondered where those two had gone. The other one left."

Dave sighed. At least Sam was safe.

"Listen, kids. I'm sorry you got into this," Tony said.

"Where's Leroy?" Rita yelled. "Where's my brother?" She began to struggle.

Leroy Is Missing

"Better tie them up, Slouch, Tony," the Short Man said.

"Is that necessary?" Tony asked. "They're just kids." Slouch gave him a nasty look and Tony shut up.

"Anyway, what's Leroy got to do with this?" Tony asked as he tied Dave's hands behind his back. "I told you I haven't seen him today."

"But you were talking about Leroy," Dave answered.

The Short Man began to laugh.

"What have you done to my brother?" Rita screamed, and tried to break out of the rope Slouch had fastened around her wrists.

"There'll be none of that. Better gag them, too," the Short Man ordered.

"Girlie, you want to know why we were talking about Leroy? You'll find out soon. Real soon," Slouch said.

The phone rang again. Tony answered it. "Fifty on Wipe-out. Got it." He hung up.

A sharp ping sounded somewhere above their heads. "What was that?" Slouch asked. Everyone listened tensely. But they didn't hear anything else. "You kids tip anyone off?" Slouch asked menacingly. Dave and Rita shook their heads. "'Cause if you have…" Slouch cracked the knuckles of his right hand with his left.

"I really am sorry you kids got involved in this," Tony said.

"Can it, Tony. You too, Slouch. It's starting," said the Short Man, and he switched on the TV.

8

The screen lit up and the picture zoomed into focus. It was the starting gate of a racetrack. The jockeys were mounting the horses.

"In this fifth race of the day, the favorite is Wipeout, with competition from Marengo and Patsy's Pride..." the announcer was saying.

Oh, no. Bookies. We're in trouble now, thought Dave.

Rita's eyes grew large. "*Mmm Mmmm*," she yelled from behind her gag. "Juss a Mmm."

"Will you cut out that buzzing?" Slouch said irritably.

"The horses are at the gate..." the announcer said.

"*Mmmm*. Juss a Mmm," Rita buzzed again.

The Short Man turned to her. "Just a minute, it sounds like she's..."

Rita began to nod her head frantically. "*Mmmm mmmm*. Juss a Mmm, Juss a Mmmm."

Leroy Is Missing

"And they're off," the announcer said.

The Short Man was up in a flash. He tugged off Rita's gag.

"That's it! Just a Minute!" she gasped. "Bet on Just a Minute!"

"Wipe-out is in the lead, with Marengo and Patsy's Pride close behind, followed by Falstaff, Just a Minute, Touché and Kelly Green."

"Go Wipe-out!" yelled Tony.

"That kid's crazy. Just a Minute is way behind in the middle of the pack and..."

"He's going to win. The horse is a closer. It doesn't matter where he is until he hits the stretch—he puts on speed in the last furlong. And he runs best when the track is hard and fast."

"No way," one of the other men said.

The announcer's voice blared out, "Wipe-out is still in the lead, but here comes Just a Minute on the outside. He's passing Marengo and Patsy's Pride..."

"Go Just a Minute!" Rita yelled. "Go! You can do it!"

"They're neck and neck. It's Wipe-out and Just a Minute. Wipe-out and Just a Minute. And the winner is Just a Minute by a nose!"

Everyone, including Dave, turned to stare at Rita, who had a huge grin plastered across her face.

Leroy Is Missing

"Well, girlie, welcome to the Killerdiller Gang," said the Short Man.

"The Killerdiller Gang!" gasped Dave.

The Short Man smiled. "I see you've heard of us. We've only the equestrian operation here. The Gang has many...departments." The Short Man turned back to Rita, who was no longer grinning. "And now," he said, "how about if you and I have a nice chat. A nice, long chat. Untie them, Tony."

9

Sam wished the sidewalk would open up and swallow him. Leroy was still missing. Dave and Rita were inside a pizzeria that was more than just a normal pizzeria. If they aren't trapped already, they probably soon will be, thought Sam, and it's my fault. And here I am free and I can't do a darn thing to help them. Detective, hah! Maybe I should get help...but they might leave while I'm getting it and then what would happen? I'm useless, totally useless. Sam dejectedly kicked a pebble. It swerved to the left. He kicked it again, hard. It bounced against a vent with a metallic ring. "What was that?" Sam heard a rough voice rise from the vent. Quickly, he knelt down and tried to look in, hoping

that no one would pass by and ask him what he was doing. He couldn't see anything, but he heard Slouch threaten Rita and his brother, and the Short Man shut Slouch up. Then he heard a voice that sounded like an announcer's. Whatever he was saying wasn't clear until Tony yelled, "Go Wipe-out!" followed by Rita hollering, "Go Just a Minute!" soon after. What the.... Why is Rita talking.... It sounds like they're.... Then, loud and clear, Sam heard the announcer say, "And the winner is Just a Minute by a nose!" It's a horse race, Sam realized. They must be taking bets down there. And Rita's horse won. She's either a lucky guesser or some kind of genius. If she's a genius, she'd be awfully useful to bookies. And if she isn't, they might get annoyed. Either way it's bad news. Oh, man, I've got to help them. There's got to be a way. There's just got to be.

10

"It's simple, really. I keep notes on certain horses. I don't have my notebook with me, but if you'd let me go home and get it..."

"You ain't going nowhere, girlie," Slouch said.

Leroy Is Missing

"I'm afraid he's right," Tony said to Rita. "You know too much about horses and about our...er... operation here. The Boss would have us...er...removed if we let you go."

"Is that what you did to Leroy?" Dave asked. "Removed him?"

"Leroy? Ah yes, you've been asking about Leroy." The Short Man turned to Rita. "Surely you know by now about Leroy."

Rita looked puzzled. Then, it dawned on her what he was talking about. "Le Roi!" she exclaimed. "It's pronounced *Le Roi*!"

"Huh?" said Slouch.

"Correct," said the Short Man. "But these yobbos aren't so refined, so he's Leroy to them. They don't even spell his name right.'"

"What are you talking about?" Dave asked.

"Le Roi. Leroy. He's a horse and I guess he was scratched from the last race—that means he wasn't able to run for some reason or another."

"Right," said Slouch, pleased that he now knew what was going on.

"So where is Leroy, your brother?" asked Dave.

He and Rita looked from the Short Man to Tony to the other men in the room. There was no response.

"Leroy, your brother?" said Slouch finally. "Never heard of him."

Leroy Is Missing

"Oh, great! We got into all this trouble for nothing," said Dave.

"Not for nothing. I think this young lady here might make us all very rich," said the Short Man.

Just what I wanted to be, rich and kidnapped, thought Dave.

Rita, thinking the same thing, gave him a sad smile.

11

Sam was frantic. He stared around wildly. I've got to get in there, I've just go to. But how? Maybe the back door. He ran around to the rear of the building where there was a parking lot. But the back door was locked, too. And then Sam saw the answer—a metal hatch cover set into the sidewalk. Could it possibly be unlocked? And if it were, then what? Would it lead him straight into the arms of those men in the basement or was there more than one room below the pizzeria? Sam knelt and put his ear to the hatch, but he heard nothing. A couple of people were entering the parking lot, heading for their car. Sam jumped to his feet and tried to look nonchalant.

Leroy Is Missing

He waited until the people drove away. I've got to risk it, he said to himself. And, taking hold of the iron ring set in the hatch cover, he pulled carefully. The heavy metal slab rose. When it was about a foot high, Sam peered in, but he couldn't see anything. He opened the hatch fully. Stairs and darkness and distant noises. Well, at least I'm not walking right into them, he thought. Slowly, stealthily, he moved down the stairs.

He was in some sort of storage room. The light trickling in showed him that much. There were sacks of flour, cans of tomato sauce. He wondered if he should close the hatch and decided against it. The voices were louder and coming from beyond a door at the far end of the room. He heard Rita yell, "Go, Happy Lady!" Now what do I do? He took a few shuffling steps forward. It was hard to see. I better feel along the walls. He moved to the right side of the room and inched his way along the wall. I still don't know what I'm doing, he thought. His hand touched a cool pipe that ran up the wall. A water pipe, probably, he thought. Suddenly, like a raindrop striking the surface of a lake, something pinged in the back of his mind. Something about water. Water, water everywhere.

"And it's Happy Lady!" the announcer's voice rang out. "We'll be back in a minute with the final race of the day..."

42

Leroy Is Missing

Final race, thought Sam, I've got to do something quick. He groped further along the wall and tried to think. What is it about water? Water and basements. Our basement at home once flooded because a pipe broke. What if I were to break a pipe? Yeah, that's it. No. No, it isn't. Even if I had something to break it with, it would take a long time to flood the basement, and anyway the water would only come up to their ankles and not over their heads!

Over their heads! Wait a minute. Basements have boilers and supplies. If a fire started, it would have to be put out fast or the whole building would go up in flames. The fastest way to put it out would be pour water on it. Water pouring down from somewhere. From…from a sprinkler system. That's it, if there's a sprinkler system here, maybe I could give those thugs a big surprise. If only I could see better.

He pulled out the pocket flashlight he always carried. He flicked it on. Nothing. Darn, the battery must be dead. Lucky I always carry matches too. He struck one and shone it along the pipe. Nothing. He blew out the match as the heat reached his fingers.

He lit a second. There were only two left in the book. Darn, I'm getting sloppy, he thought, I better pay more attention to my "detective kit" from now on. He pushed the thought away and looked at the ceiling. Sure enough, there were the sprinklers. Now where, where? The match flickered and went out. He heard the announcer's voice calling out the lineup for the final race. Hurry, he told himself, lighting a third match. Check that corner.

Then, he saw it. A little metal box with an "eye." A sensor. There were probably a number of them up there.

"Ouch," he said aloud as the flame burnt his forefinger. Only one match left and I don't even know if this sensor works the sprinklers in the other room too, assuming there are sprinklers in the other room. Well, it's worth a try.

There was a convenient pile of sacks under the sensor. He climbed them. Then, he struck the last match and held it under the "eye." The match burned lower and lower, but nothing happened. "Rain, darn it, rain!" Sam whispered.

12

Suddenly, it did. The sprinklers opened full force, showering Sam and the sacks and the cans. And from the other room, he heard yells and curses and the sounds of people bumping into things. Then,

the door swung open and a bunch of people poured through, Dave and Rita among them.

"What's going on?" the Short Man shouted. "Is there a fire?"

"I don't know. I don't see anything. The sensor must be broken or something...." It was Tony. He noticed the thin stream of light across the room. "Hey, what's this?"

Sam went into action. "Rita, Dave!" he hollered, jumping down from the sacks onto Tony's back. "Hurry! The hatch!"

Rita pivoted and shoved the Short Man against Slouch. They fell to the floor and she streaked for the stairs. Dave almost stumbled over Tony, but he managed to right himself.

"Sam, where are you?" he called.

"Coming!" Sam rolled off Tony and leaped to his feet.

But Slouch was there, grabbing him. Sam pulled an old trick and chomped down on the man's arm. "*Oww!*" he yelled.

"Hey, Mikey, grab that kid," Slouch bellowed at one of the other men.

"No, sir. I don't hold with mistreating kids."

Rita was already in the street. Dave was climbing the last steps. Sam pulled a case of cans down and sent them rolling under the feet of the Short Man,

who'd managed to get up. Down he went again, and up the stairs went Sam.

"The police station!" gasped Dave.

"Oh, no you don't," growled a voice. It was Slouch, thundering up the stairs.

"Please, kids, stop and nobody'll get hurt," Tony pleaded, also charging up the stairs.

"Hurry!" yelled Sam.

And off they went, Slouch, Tony and the Short Man hot on their heels.

They raced down Johnson Street to Rackley Road. Rita banged into an old man who shook his cane at her. Sam almost knocked over a baby carriage. People gave them dirty looks. "Kids," one woman sneered. What does she think of the grown-ups running after us, Sam thought, but in this town, nothing seems to surprise anyone. He looked behind him and noticed that only Slouch was still pursuing them. Tony and the Short Man were gone. That's strange, Sam thought. Then Dave twisted his ankle. Slouch gained on him and grabbed for his arm.

"Quick! This way!" Sam yelled, ducking into an alley next to Stimson's Toy Store. Rita and Dave followed. "Quick, this'll take us to…" Sam didn't finish his sentence. Blocking the end of the alley were Tony and the Short Man. And the Short Man was looking real mean. Sam spun around to go

back the way he came, but Slouch was already there.

"Well, well, so good to see you again so soon," said the Short Man. "I think we'll have that chat now. All six of us. But in more comfortable surroundings than this. You picked a convenient meeting place. Our van is just around the corner. Now, this way, lady and gentlemen. We will escort you." The Short Man motioned with his hand and Slouch shoved Sam in the back.

"You heard it, kid. Move!" he barked.

Sam looked at Dave, then at Rita. "I'm sorry," he said.

"It's not your fault."

"For leading us into this alley..."

"Hey, brother, you tried your best to..." Dave began.

"Enough of this mutual admiration society. Let's go!" the Short Man ordered.

"Mutual admiration society? Are they bookies too?" Slouch asked.

The Short Man shook his head in disgust and waved his hand once more. Sam, Dave and Rita started walking out of the alley.

Leroy Is Missing

13

Just then, the back door to Stimson's Toy Store opened. Out stepped a trim, well-dressed, middle-aged man with bushy eyebrows, who looked familiar to Sam, and a small, red-haired, freckle-faced boy.

"Leroy!" yelled Rita.

"Leroy!" echoed Sam and Dave.

"Where have you been? We've looked all over for you."

"Ah, it's the famous Leroy at last," the Short Man said.

"I've been here. In Stimson's with Uncle Doug. I'm just walking him to his car in the lot around the corner," Leroy answered Rita. Then he noticed Slouch, Tony and the Short Man, who had moved very fast and was holding Rita around the neck. "Hey, what's going on here? You guys being kidnapped or something?"

"A bright boy, your brother," said the Short Man. "I'm afraid, young man, 'you guys' now includes you and your Uncle Doug."

Leroy Is Missing

"Uncle Doug!" Rita exclaimed. *"This* is Uncle Doug? But who is he?"

Before Uncle Doug could answer, Slouch spoke up. "I know who he is. I watch him on TV all the time. He's the best yo-yo expert in the world!"

"On television! At Mr. Treebottom's. That's where I saw you!" Sam exclaimed.

"I never watch TV," Rita muttered.

"But what are you doing here?" asked Dave.

This time, Uncle Doug got to answer. He pulled two yo-yos out of his pockets and nervously began to twirl them. "I was on my way to give a demonstration at Midday Camp this evening. I met Leroy here, who watches my show…"

"Every week!" Leroy said excitedly. "I asked him to show me some tricks—'Walking the Dog' and 'Going Over the Mountain' and…"

"Going over the mountain!" Dave looked at Sam and the two of them groaned.

"Yeah…and he showed them to me," Leroy finished.

"Yo-yos! I love yo-yos!" Slouch said.

Everyone looked surprised.

Then, Sam got an idea. "Dave and I like yo-yos, too. We used to play with them," he said.

"Yeah, we were pretty good, too," put in Dave.

Sam smiled briefly. He hoped Dave was reading

his mind as he sometimes did. "Could you maybe show us a trick?" Sam asked.

"Oh, no you don't. Quit stalling for..." the Short Man began.

But Slouch interrupted him. "Please, Boss. It'll only take a few minutes."

"Yeah," said Tony. "Let him do it."

The Short Man was outnumbered. "Oh, all right," he sighed. "But remember, try anything funny, I've got the girl here and my van is just around the corner."

Uncle Doug was happy to oblige. He showed them "Walking the Dog" and "Going Over the Mountain" and a few other tricks. Everyone applauded (except the Short Man, who didn't want to let go of Rita). Then Sam said, "There was a special trick Dave and I used to do. It's called 'The Lariat.'"

Dave's face lit up. "Oh, that's a good one," he said.

Uncle Doug looked blankly at Sam for a moment. "*Hmmm*, that's a new one on me. I'd like to see it. One or two yo-yos?"

"Four," said Sam. "Two for me and two for Dave."

"Hey, I don't like this," said the Short Man.

"Leroy, lend this young man your yo-yos, please," Uncle Doug said, handing his two to Sam.

Leroy Is Missing

"I said I don't like this..."

"Aww, Boss, let 'em finish. They're almost *finished* anyway." Slouch snorted at his crude joke.

"Do I have to lend him my yo-yos?" Leroy began to whine. "He'll mess them up..."

Rita cut him off with a shout. "Give him those yo-yos or I'll make sure you'll never see your bicycle again!"

Leroy made a face, but dug the yo-yos out of his pockets and tossed them to Dave.

"You ready?" Sam asked.

"Ready," said Dave.

"Okay, then. One. Two. Three."

What happened next was over so fast no one really saw it, only the result.

Sam and Dave shot out their yo-yos and wrapped them around Tony's and the Short Man's feet. The Short Man fell to the ground and Rita quickly broke away from him. Dave also tried to encircle Slouch's feet, but he missed. Slouch lunged forward, but Rita stuck out her foot and neatly tripped him. Slouch hit the ground with a thud and stayed there. Sam quickly tied up the Short Man's hands firmly with the yo-yos. Dave tied up Tony. And Rita found a length of twine in a garbage can and got to work on Slouch.

"Leroy, why don't you go back into Stimson's

and ask Mr. Stimson to call the police?" Uncle Doug suggested.

For once, Leroy did as he was told.

14

"I feel kind of sorry for Tony," Sam said as he, Dave, Rita and Leroy were drinking lemonade in the O'Tooles' kitchen. The police had arrived and arrested the Short Man, Slouch and Tony and one of the other men at the pizzeria (the other one got away). "I don't think he was really part of the gang. I think he had to go along with what they told him to do."

"I think you're right," Dave said. "Maybe they'll let him off."

"Well, I think you guys are A-one detectives," said Rita.

Sam felt his heart thump. "We...I...didn't do much," he said. "You're a pretty good detective yourself."

Rita gave him a big smile. Then she turned to Leroy. "One thing I still don't understand is why Jason Rothberg didn't tell me you told him to watch your bike. Why did he pretend he found it?"

Leroy Is Missing

"Because Jason Rothberg is a chicken. He's afraid of his mother. His mother said he had to be home at noon and I wasn't back yet, and his mother doesn't want him hanging out with me, and he lied because he was afraid his mother would find out he *was* hanging out with me."

"But why doesn't Jason's mother want him hanging out with you?"

"Um...well...I beat him up a couple of times," Leroy admitted.

No one said anything. Everyone just gave Leroy a disgusted look.

"But I promised him if he watched my bike I wouldn't beat him up anymore."

"And you won't?"

"Nah. I'm going to *sue* him instead"—he pointed at Sam—"after I sue him for scratching my bike."

"Next time Leroy is missing, we'll be out of town," Sam muttered.

"Over the mountain," Dave added.

He and Sam looked at each other and slapped five.

59